The Three Little Pigs

and me!

For Thomas and Matthew – E.B.

First published 2015 by Nosy Crow Ltd
The Crow's Nest, 10a Lant Street
London SE1 1QR
www.nosycrow.com
ISBN 978 0 85763 469 6 (HB)
ISBN 978 0 85763 045 2 (PB)
Nosy Crow and associated logos are trademarks
and/or registered trademarks of Nosy Crow Ltd
Text © Nosy Crow 2015
Illustrations © Nosy Crow 2011
The right of Ed Bryan to be identified as the
illustrator of this work has been asserted.

The Three Little Pigs

 nosy crow

Illustrated by
Ed Bryan

Once upon a time, there
were **three little pigs**.

The time came for the little pigs to **leave** their home and make their way in the world.

"**Goodbye,** my little ones! Be happy, but beware of the **Big Bad Wolf,**" said their mother.

And so the **three little pigs** went on their way.

The **first** little pig found a piece of land and he quickly built himself a house made of **straw.**

The **second** little pig found a piece of land and
she quickly built herself a house made of **sticks**.

The **third** little pig
decided to build a house
made of **bricks**.

He worked **hard** and his house took a **long** time to build.

The three little pigs lived **happily** in their three little houses until, one day, the **Big Bad Wolf** arrived in the neighbourhood.

BANG!

BANG!

BANG!

The wolf knocked at the door
of the **first** little pig.

"Little pig, little pig, may I **come in?**" said the Big Bad Wolf.

"Not by the **hair** on my chinny chin **chin!**" said the first little pig.

"Then I'll **huff** and I'll **puff** and I'll **blow** your house down!" growled the wolf.

So the Big Bad Wolf **huffed** and he **puffed** and he blew the house **down**.

And the little pig ran **squealing** to his sister's house with the wolf **racing** after him.

The Big Bad Wolf knocked at the
door of the **second** little pig.

BANG!

BANG!

BANG!

"Little pig, little pig, may I come in?"
"Not by the **hair** on my chinny chin **chin!**"
said the second little pig.

"Then I'll **huff** . . .

and I'll **puff** . . .

and I'll **blow** your house down!"
growled the wolf.

So the Big Bad Wolf huffed and he **puffed** and he blew the house **down.**

And the little pigs ran **squealing** to their brother's house with the wolf **racing** after them.

The Big Bad Wolf knocked at the door of the **third** little pig. "Little pig, little pig, may I **come in?**"

BANG!
BANG!
BANG!

"Not by the **hair** on my chinny chin **chin!**"
said the third little pig.

"Then I'll **huff** and I'll **puff** and I'll **blow** your house down!" growled the wolf.

So the Big Bad Wolf **huffed** and he **puffed**, and he huffed and he **puffed**, but the brick house **didn't** fall down.

The Big Bad Wolf was **angry** and he was **hungry.**

He climbed up onto the roof and squashed himself into the **chimney.**

The moment the third little pig heard the wolf's big feet on the roof, he knew **exactly** what to do . . .

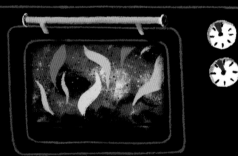

. . . and he put a
very big pot of water
on the cooker to boil.

Then, just as the Big Bad Wolf slid down
the chimney, the little pig pulled the
lid off the pot of hot water . . .

. . . and in dropped the wolf!

The Big Bad Wolf burned his bottom **very** badly and ran **howling** down the road. He was never, **ever** seen again!

And the three little pigs lived
happily ever after.